# Words to Know Before You Read

Let's Learn The
**bl, br**
Sound

blimp
blow
blue
Bluefield Blazers
Brad
Bret
bridge
brown

www.rourkeeducationalmedia.com

Edited by Precious McKenzie
Illustrated by Ed Myer
Art Direction and Page Layout by Tara Raymo
Cover Design by Renee Brady

**Library of Congress PCN Data**

A Blimp in the Blue / J. Jean Robertson
ISBN 978-1-62169-270-6 (hard cover) (alk. paper)
ISBN 978-1-62169-228-7 (soft cover)
Library of Congress Control Number: 2012952775

Rourke Educational Media
Printed in the United States of America,
North Mankato, Minnesota

rourkeeducationalmedia.com

customerservice@rourkeeducationalmedia.com • PO Box 643328 Vero Beach, Florida 32964

# A Blimp in the Blue

Counselor
Brad

Counselor
Soni

Counselor
Fred

Captain
Karl

Bret

Andee

Willa

Effie

Cole

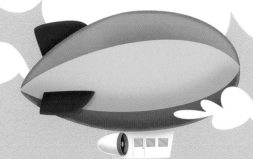

Written By J. Jean Robertson
Illustrated By Ed Myer

Counselor Brad calls, "All aboard the bus if you want to see a blimp."

CAMP ADV

BLIMP HANGAR

CAMP ADVENTURE

5

"Do they keep the blimp in a garage?" asks Willa.

"Maybe in a big barn," says Cole.

Counselor Soni says, "They are kept in buildings called hangars."

CAMP ADVENTUR

As the bus bumps across a big bridge, Cole asks, "How much farther?"

"Look out the window," says Willa. "What do you see?" she asks.

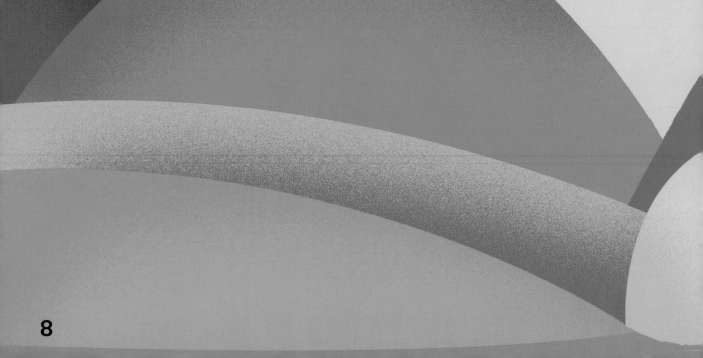

"Oh! Wow! There's a big, brown building!" yells Bret.

"It must be the biggest building in the whole world!" says Effie.

"Maybe it's a blimp hangar," says Cole.

Counselor Fred calls out, "I want you to meet Captain Karl."

"Hello! You may ask questions as we look at the blimp," says Captain Karl.

Andee says, "I saw a blimp at the Bluefield Blazers baseball game, but it didn't seem so big."

"It looks much bigger when you are right beside it," says Captain Karl.

"Could our big bus ride in it?" asks Bret.

"Not in the big part," says Captain Karl.

"We call the big part the envelope. It is filled with helium, like a balloon. People ride in the gondola."

Captain Karl tells them, "Blimps have engines and propellers. Pilots can control where they go. They don't need to wait for the wind to blow. Let's hop in and fly."

They fly high in the big, blue sky. They fly over a bridge, a barn, and a bus.

Cole looks out the window and says, "We're high up in the blue sky! Our bus looks like a tiny toy!"

# After Reading Word Study

## Picture Glossary

Directions: Look at each picture and read the definition. Write a list of all of the words you know that start with the same sound as *blimp* or *bridge*. Remember to look in the book for more words.

**blimp** (BLIMP): A blimp is an airship. People ride in the gondola.

**blow** (BLOH): To move the air or when the wind moves.

 **blue** (BLOO): The color of the sky on a sunny day.

 **Brad** (BRAD): A man or boy's name. Sometimes it is short for Bradley.

 **bridge** (BRIJ): A structure built over a river or road. It helps people cross to the other side.

 **brown** (BROUN): The color of coffee or chocolate.

# About the Author

J. Jean Robertson, also known as Bushka to her grandchildren and many other kids, lives in San Antonio, Florida with her husband. She is retired after many years of teaching. She remembers first seeing a blimp at Tillamook, Oregon, during the Second World War.

**Ask The Author!**
www.rem4students.com

# About the Illustrator

Ed Myer is a Manchester-born illustrator now living in London. After growing up in an artistic household, Ed studied ceramics at university but always continued drawing pictures. As well as illustration, Ed likes traveling, playing computer games, and walking little Ted (his Jack Russell).

CSCL

## DATE DUE